SEARCH FOR THE LOST TOOTH

By Maria S. Barbo

Illustrated by Duendes del Sur

ABDOPUBLISHING.COM

Reinforced library bound edition published in 2017 by Spotlight, a division of ABDO. PO Box 398166, Minneapolis, Minnesota 55439. Spotlight produces high-quality reinforced library bound editions for schools and libraries. Published by agreement with Warner Bros. Entertainment Inc.

Printed in the United States of America, North Mankato, Minnesota.
042016   092016

THIS BOOK CONTAINS
RECYCLED MATERIALS

PUBLISHER'S CATALOGING IN PUBLICATION DATA

Names: Barbo, Maria S., author. | Duendes del Sur, illustrator.
Title: Scooby-Doo and the search for the lost tooth / by Maria S. Barbo ; illustrated by Duendes del Sur.
Description: Minneapolis, MN : Spotlight, [2017] | Series: Scooby-Doo early reading adventures
Summary: Scooby and Shaggy are playing with their friend Billy when his tooth mysteriously goes missing! Did a monster really take Billy's tooth? It's up to Scooby to solve the mystery and find Billy's lost tooth.
Identifiers: LCCN 2016930653 | ISBN 9781614794721 (lib. bdg.)
Subjects: LCSH: Scooby-Doo (Fictitious character)--Juvenile fiction. | Teeth--Juvenile fiction. | Ghosts--Juvenile fiction. | Mystery and detective stories--Juvenile fiction. | Adventure and adventurers--Juvenile fiction.
Classification: DDC [Fic]--dc23
LC record available at http://lccn.loc.gov/2016930653

Spotlight
A Division of ABDO
abdopublishing.com

It was a great day!

Scooby and the gang were playing at their friend Billy's house.

Fred, Velma and Daphne played volleyball.

Scooby and Shaggy took a break to snack on pizza and apples.

Scooby and Shaggy saw Billy

sitting on the porch all alone.

"What's wrong?" Shaggy

asked him.

"I lost my tooth," Billy said.

"Like, that's great!" Shaggy

said. "Maybe the tooth fairy will

come visit you."

"But I don't know where my

tooth is," Billy said.

"Like, no prob," Shaggy said.

"Scoob and I will find your

tooth!"

Scooby and Shaggy went to look
for Billy's tooth in the yard.
They heard a noise that went
clankedy, clank, whir, whir.
"Zoinks! What's that noise?"
asked Shaggy.
"Ronster!" yelped Scooby.
Billy wondered if a monster
could have taken his tooth.

Shaggy told Billy to retrace his steps.

"Before I lost my tooth, I was playing in the grass by the pool," said Billy.

Scooby dug some holes in the grass.

He found flowers and dirt…and more dirt.

He did not find Billy's tooth.

Then they heard the funny noise.

Clankedy, clank, whir, whir.

"Run!" yelled Shaggy. "It's the monster!"

Scooby, Shaggy and Billy ran to the picnic table.

Billy's mother had set out some cake and milk.

Scooby and Shaggy were very hungry from searching for the tooth.

They gobbled down the cake and drank all the milk.

Billy could see that finding his tooth was hard work.

Billy tried to remember the other places where he had played. "Before I played in the grass, I went down the slide," Billy said. "Reee!" Scooby slid down the slide.

He did not find Billy's tooth.

Then Scooby and Shaggy heard the funny noise again.

Clankedy, clank, whir, whir.

"Rikes!" yelled Scooby.

"Let's get out of here!" said Shaggy.

Scooby hopped on Billy's bike and they sped off away from the monster.

"What else were you doing before you lost your tooth?" asked Shaggy.

"I was eating an apple," said Billy.

Shaggy looked at the apple. He did not see the missing tooth.

"I played with my favorite toy robot too," Billy said.

Just then, they heard the noise.

Clankedy, clank, whir, whir.

"It's the monster! Run!" Shaggy said.

Scooby and Shaggy bumped into Velma and knocked off her glasses.

Clankedy, clank, whir, whir.

"Jinkies!" yelled Velma. "What is that noise?"

"That's the monster!" Shaggy said.

Fred and Daphne came running to see what had happened.

Shaggy and Scooby hid behind a bush.

Velma put her glasses back on.

"That's not a monster," said Billy. "It's my toy robot!"

"And the toy was carrying your tooth," said Velma.

"Hooray!" said Billy. "Now I can put my tooth under my pillow for the tooth fairy."

Everyone was proud of Scooby and Shaggy.

Daphne gave them some Scooby-Snacks.

"Thanks for helping me find my tooth," Billy said.

"Scooby-Dooby-Doo!" barked Scooby.

The End